CALLUM'S BIG DAY

TOM POW

Illustrated by
Mairi Hedderwick

ιυγξ

iynx publishing

'You are invited to a **BIG PARTY**
at my house,' Callum wrote
one day to all his friends.

'**DRESS SCOTTISH**,'
the invitation said.

Tristan

Martha

Ailsa

Sophie

Louis

Joe

Sam

Jean

Omar

Anh

Kirsty

Rashid

Li

Cameron

Jasveer

Jenny

Ewan

Callum wanted to be a
REAL Scotsman like he'd seen in the films.
So his Dad bought him a kilt.

He told Callum he'd grow into it.

His Granny knitted him a beard
(she told him he'd grow into it)

and a Scottie dog
which he called Taggart.

He would have called the dog
Hamish —

if Hamish wasn't the name he'd given
his sister. Her name was Sophie.

"Stop calling me Hamish," she said.
"*And NO, I don't want a wee dram.*"

"You're going bonkers!" she told him.

But Callum was determined.
He learned to say the Selkirk Grace —
even when it was spaghetti for tea —

and to dance the Highland Fling
when everyone was trying
to watch the TV.
"Bonkers!" said Sophie again. *"Bonkers!"*

His Uncle Harry made him a sword —
just like William Wallace's. Uncle Harry
had measured it specially in a museum
and wrapped it as a surprise.

Springtime is
Daffodil time

Yellow

'Sam   Sophie   Martha   Jenny

"Well, what colour *is* a daffodil?"
asked his teacher.
"Ach, Ah dinna ken ocht aboot
daffies," said Callum,
the Highland Warrior —

who, at night, slept on a bed of thistles
in his feathered bunnet
and dreamed of fighting beside Bruce
at Bannockburn —

and with Bonnie Prince Charlie at Culloden. Aye, and winning this time!

"I'm worried Callum's taking this all a bit too seriously," his Dad said to his Mum one day, as Callum finished his cornflakes, wiped his woollen beard and said, "Aye, Ah like a drap o' guid porritch."

an' we can eat
be thankit.

Then the day arrived.
The day that, all this time,
Callum had been preparing for.

"Right, Dad!" Callum said.
"Now I'm ready!"

Ready for...

THE BIG PARTY